AF418014

# RESCUING REYA

FLORIDA VETERANS
BOOK 6

TIFFANI LYNN

*This is for all those people who loved and lost but were strong enough to open their hearts again. May you find every happiness you ever hoped for.*

# 1

## REYA

If I'd known today was going to be the last one like it, I never would've taken it all for granted. Sometimes, though, it's better you don't see what's coming.

THE WIND TOSSES LITTLE WISPS OF MY HAIR AROUND MY FACE while my sunglasses protect my eyes as Alex hits the throttle. Every Sunday, for as long as we've been together, we're on his bike riding down all the back roads this part of Texas has to offer. During these moments I always feel so young and free with my arms wrapped tight around his middle. Today is no different until he pulls off the road behind an old run-down gas station and kills the engine.

"Why are we stopping? This place is kinda creepy." We never pull off at these kinds of places.

"We're being followed," he says as he climbs off the bike. "I'm hoping they keep going. I tried to lose them around the last bend in the road. I didn't see them when we pulled in."

"Followed by whom?" I ask, wondering what he's talking about.

"I'm in a little trouble, honey," he says, like using that little term of endearment at the end will make it better.

Alex's nervous pacing and the sudden sweat above his brow tells me he's freaked out. This isn't some little thing; whatever it is, it's bad.

"What kind of trouble?"

"I have video footage that I shouldn't have. I did it for the right reasons, though."

What the hell kind of footage would have us being followed? This sounds like the plot of some movie. "Well, get rid of it. I don't care what it is, if you're in trouble, dump it."

"I can't. I've got proof that these dudes from Detroit are selling people here in Texas."

"What?" My eyes bulge out of my head. "Human trafficking? Oh my God! Alex..."

"Listen, I'm going to make it right. We aren't out on our normal Sunday ride. We're meeting a guy right outside of Kerrville in thirty minutes to turn over the evidence. He's with the FBI and he'll know what to do with it. Just in case something happens, though, I want you to know that I love you, more than anything."

My breathe catches and my chest tightens. "But—" I'm ready to ask a thousand questions and he knows me too well to know it's going to happen.

He leans in close and brushes his lips across mine lingering there long enough to say, "Not now. If we make it out of here I'll tell you everything. We have to go. These guys are in a black van so we have to make sure we lose them completely before we get to Donovan. Once we're on the bike, hold on tight." He kisses me hard and fast one last time.

Fear like I've never known courses through me as I climb on behind him on to his Harley-Davidson Street Glide. Usually I love this bike, but right now it feels like a death trap. If we're running from someone, I want a vehicle that's more like a tank to protect us. We're right out in the open on this thing. Why is he being so irresponsible? I can't believe he brought me along for this.

As I lower the helmet onto my head and wrap my body around his, I think about all that is Alex. I've been in love with him since freshman year of college when he charmed me right out of my biology notes. He was born with a charisma that few people have and he used it to his full advantage when he was trying to get my attention. I fought it for a while, but eventually gave in. The day I graduated with my BSN he asked me to marry him and we got married the following year with all the hoopla a huge wedding is expected to have. That was two years ago.

Alex has always been the life of the party and the man everyone seems to know and love. We can't ever go to dinner or a movie without him having to stop and talk to several people. What I don't understand is how he could get wrapped up in something as sinister as this. Sure, he's turning evidence over to the FBI, but how did he end up with it in the first place?

Now I wish I'd been around more. I've been working six days a week for the last three months. I'm a hospice nurse and we've been short-staffed. Nursing in general is difficult. Six days a week dealing with dying patients and their families wears on me, so by the time I get home I don't have a lot left over. I thought in a couple months, once we get all the new people hired and trained, I could take a week off so Alex and I could go somewhere and reconnect, to catch up on everything and start working on making a family again. But now I realize I should have tuned in sooner.

A few minutes back into our ride, Alex starts whipping in and out of traffic and passing people every chance he gets. He's driving like a maniac and my knuckles are white because I'm holding on so tight. He peels off down a back road that we rarely travel and hits the throttle again. I grip his middle tighter and pray as hard as I can that we walk away from this.

He looks back over his shoulder and cusses loudly before passing two cars and speeding up. We're going around a bend when Alex crosses the double yellow line to pass the car in front of us and I glance up, ready to cuss him out, when I see the semi coming straight at us. He swerves and heads off the road. The last sound I hear is the blaring of the truck's horn and my own scream as we drive straight into a tree and my world goes black.

2

——————

**REYA**

STUMBLING OUT OF THE BATHROOM I MAKE A ZIGZAG PATTERN across the room. I think it's safe to say I've had too much to drink. If I didn't know it before I went in there, I do now. After almost falling in the toilet, soaking my shirt while washing my hands, and then crashing into a woman on the way out, I have no illusions about my intoxicated status.

It's the anniversary of the accident and I can't seem to hide from the ghosts flying around in my head. Even after a year it all feels like yesterday and I can't live with any of the memories of Alex or the aftermath. Drinking seemed like a good way to shut those things down for the night.

With a heavy sigh I plop back down on my barstool and tap the bar top. The bartender, whose name is Bud, or so he tells me, plants both hands on the edge of the bar and leans down to make close eye contact. "Lady, you don't need anything else to drink."

"I'm not driving. I'm staying across the street. Shouldn't matter how much I drink if I'm not driving."

"I don't need ya dyin' of alcohol poisonin' after I served it to you."

"I know when to cut this off. I promise. This time, though, I want a shot of your best whiskey. In fact, serve one up to these guys too." I gesture to the line of three mostly toothless, scraggly bearded men who appear to live on these stools night after night. "This one's on me," I yell to the guys thrusting my arms in the air, and they all cheer. Bud shakes his head but lines up the shot glasses to fill them with the amber liquid.

"Wait for me to do it, boys, okay?" I shout at them over the noise of the jukebox. They all look at me like I've lost my mind. "This is the important part," I inform them.

Then I shuffle over to the jukebox and fish a wadded-up dollar bill out of my pocket and do my best to flatten it out. When the jukebox won't take it, my frustration mounts and I bang my head on the machine. I need to get this song on now. It's the song that goes with the shot. This is how he always did this shot.

"Hey, hey, hey, lady, cut that out. You break it and Bud won't replace it. We'll be stuck listening to Big John tell stories about the good ole days," grumbles a male voice with a heavy southern accent.

I lift my head and do my best to focus on the guy scolding me. Where'd he come from? He doesn't look like the other locals. First of all, he's younger, closer to my age. He's also wearing a worn white cowboy hat and has a day's worth of blond stubble. He's a few inches taller than I am, which puts him right under six foot, I bet. His face has a rugged quality that I'd only associate with tough men, but it's still handsome enough that I have to fight the drunken instinct to touch his cheeks.

"I have to play this song. It's important, but it won't take my money," I tell him, noticing a bit of a slur at the end of most of my words. *Shit.*

"Lady, I'll put money in there and get your song pulled up if you agree not to bang your pretty little head on it again."

I nod a little and shove the dollar at him. Mr. Cowboy shakes his head and says, "No ma'am. I've got this. You tell me your song and head back to the bar."

"Bob Seger, 'Roll Me Away'."

"Seger?" His eyebrows rise and his head tilts a little. "No, Miranda Lambert or Carrie Underwood?" He teases like he doesn't believe me. Normally, I'd find this funny, but not this time. It's important to me to get it right for Alex. "Nope, just the Seger," I tell him sadly and return to the bar.

The shots are still sitting there waiting so I tell the boys on the stools to grab one each and then I hold the shot up high like Alex always did and say loudly, "Here's to you and here's to me. If we should ever disagree, fuck you and here's to me!" I lift mine higher and declare, "This one's for Alex!"

"Ma'am, ain't no Alex in here," Bud tells me with a lifted brow before we can toss them back. Everyone pauses, seeming to want to know what I'm going to say.

"No," I reply, and pound my chest with my fist directly over my heart. "He's in here. Now, let me get back to this." I put the shot glass to my lips and turn it upside down, letting the liquid burn a path down my throat to my stomach.

The guys with the shots lift them toward me and then throw them back. My eyes close so I can picture my Alex, with his alluring charisma, doing what I just did, probably a hundred times in the years we were together. I stay that way until the first notes of the song float out of the speakers, then I turn and move to the dance floor and slide into my own private world, one where I'm on the back of Alex's bike before I worked too many hours and he met the wrong people. Before my whole world imploded. The music takes me away and I'm singing at the top of my lungs and dancing the awkward dance of sad, drunken women all over the world.

When the song finally fades out, I open my eyes to find everyone in the place looking at me. This would normally embarrass me, but not tonight. Drunk, sad, lonely and done reminiscing, I drag myself back to the bar and slap a hundred-dollar bill up there for Bud and shuffle out of the building.

Bud calls to me as I go, "This is too much, honey!"

I wave my hand in the air dismissing his words and keep going. When I step outside into the cold Florida night I blink a few times at the shock of it. Damn, it's freezing here. I've never been to this part of the country so I had no idea that it gets cold here at times. I glance at the old neon sign across the street that says Martha Ann's Motel and begin my short trek back to my room.

On the whole walk over I contemplate all that's going on. How did my life end up such a mess? Alex was my glue and the minute he became a bunch of pieces on the side of the road, so did my life.

I dig down in my pocket and pull out the old-school metal key on the plastic diamond-shaped keyring. Then I drag my drunk ass to the door marked number three. Earlier in the evening I picked this place because I knew no one would be looking for me here. In fact, if I had to guess, no one has ever looked here for anyone. This place is a total dump. It was probably built in the 1950's and never updated. I'm certain the furniture and mattress were installed right after it was built. This is not the Disney World part of Florida with perfect landscaping and cookie cutter homes. It's the kind that Hollywood executives find to film some terrifying scary movie in where inbreeding has been going on for years and none of the living structures get cited by the government as being uninhabitable because then no one would live here. It's the perfect place to hide. I lean my head against the door and take a deep breath. It may take me a minute to focus enough to get the key in the hole the right way, but I'm ready to try.

As I fight with the key and the lock, I realize it probably wasn't smart to get this drunk when I should be watching my back. The battle continues for a few minutes until I finally give up. My shoulders sag in defeat and I'm ready to go to the office for help when I hear Mr. Cowboy's voice way too close behind me. My brain is too foggy to be startled.

"Doll, looks like you need some help."

Great, this is so humiliating; he's either here to laugh at my stupid inebriated state or kill me. It didn't dawn on me until just now that he could be one of the assholes making my life a living hell. I doubt it, since the guys I'm dealing with are from Detroit, not some cow pasture in the middle of nowhere, but by getting drunk I left myself vulnerable. What an idiot. I'm so tired of dealing with all of this, especially since I didn't do anything to deserve it. I survived, that's my transgression.

"If you're here to kill me, please get it over with. I'm tired of running."

"Lady, I don't know what the hell you're talking about, but if you're in danger, hanging out here in the open, so drunk you can barely stand, is a shitty way to stay safe." He grips my shoulders and turns me toward him, searching my face, for what, I don't know. The blue in his eyes is the only thing I can seem to focus on. It's the prettiest icy blue I've ever seen and I swear he can see straight through to my soul, to all the heartache, worry and anger I've got stored up in there.

Turning around he glances in all directions, never taking his hands off my shoulders. He pauses on something at the back of the lot, but I don't look over to see what it is. I study his profile. The column of his throat is thick, his Adam's apple slightly visible. His shoulders are broad and thick like he lifts heavy weights frequently, and although it's covered, his chest is thick. If I felt it I'd probably find amazing pecs under his flannel shirt. I can't seem to help myself when I reach up and run my hands from the tops of his shoulders down his arms and back across his chest. Everything feels exactly like I expected and I sigh.

When he glances back to me his eyebrows are drawn together and I realize I never got permission to touch him and that was probably wrong. This is why I don't drink very often. Besides getting sentimental, I also get touchy-feely. He turns back to the parking lot and I go back to studying him.

"Give me the key, doll." His eyes never leave their point of interest in the parking lot as he wraps his fingers around the key in my hand and moves me to the side a little. Quickly, he opens the door and shuffles us inside. He leads me to stand in front of the big window facing the parking lot and before my alcohol soaked brain can comprehend what he's doing his lips meet mine and his arms wrap me up and hold me tight. The kiss is strong but his lips are soft and I melt a little, realizing it's been a year since I was kissed or held this way. It's so nice. Super nice. Beyond the word nice.

Abruptly he yanks the curtain closed and moves me to the bed. "Sit. You've got someone watching you out there. I wanted them to think we'll be busy for a bit. I need to make a call." He dials and holds the phone up to his ear and then asks me, "You running from the law or someone else?"

"Someone else, I guess. Dudes from Detroit."

"You kill someone or hurt a kid?"

"What?" What is this guy going on about? Me, kill someone? Never.

"Did you kill someone or hurt a kid?" he says a little slower and a little louder.

"Hell, no! Why'd you ask that?" I notice the slur again and it seems to be back worse than last time.

He shifts his focus back to the call. "Hudson, it's Elias Covington, I need your help."

"Shitty motel on route 98. Got a girl here running from some trouble and it's found her. Yup, waiting in the parking lot. My piece is in the car so I've got nothin'. Room three." He pauses, listening. "Yup, we'll be here." Then he disconnects and stares at me.

"My head's pounding. Can I lie down for a minute?"

"Don't pass out. If this guy decides to come in after you it could get hairy."

"Hairy?" I'm way more drunk than I thought I was; I can't figure out what he's talking about.

"The guy in the parking lot. You know you're being watched, right?"

My stomach rolls over. I thought I got away free and clear. How did they find me?

"You might as well leave me here and go. I can't escape it and I don't care anymore." I fall back and close my eyes to avoid watching the room spin and allow myself to drift off. I've got nothing left to live for anyway. I've cut off contact with virtually everyone I know, except my parents, because I was afraid for their lives. I'm lonely, I'm tired of being scared, and I hate what my life has become. Dying doesn't sound too bad right now.

**3**

---

## ELIAS

ow the hell did I stumble on the only woman in this little town with serious drama? Whatever is going on isn't your run-of-the-mill trouble either. The guy in the truck outside has the look of a street thug. You don't find any of those around these parts. I wish she were feeling a little more talkative so I could figure out what's going on and decide what to do. Being passed out, she's about to lose her choice in the matter. If Hudson gets here and she's still out cold, she's going over my shoulder and back to my place. I have a state-of-the-art alarm system and plenty of firepower to take out anyone who comes sniffing around her until I can figure out what the hell is going on.

I knew when I laid eyes on her in the bar that I should've stayed away from her. I have a feeling I'm going to end up regretting this, but after losing my little sister like I did, I can't walk away from a woman in need. There are so many nights I lie awake wishing someone would've been man enough to step in and help her. Of course, I was over in Afghanistan and she was in college, so there was nothing I could do. But even seven years later I can't come to terms with the fact that she died helpless and alone.

It's only ten minutes later when Hudson shows up with Mike. Hudson shoves her stuff in her suitcase and drags it to the car while I throw her over my shoulder and carry her to my truck. Mike covers us, eyes on the watcher in the truck the whole time. Once we're all loaded up, Mike and Hudson escort us to the property where I rent a room. The black truck follows at a distance. The gate to the property is electric and takes a remote or code to open it. Although it's not impossible to breach without the remote or code, it's much more difficult than driving right up to a house. I have no idea what this lady's done, but I know it's serious. When she's safe and tucked away in my bed I'll do a little digging.

———

No one came looking last night, but I don't expect it to be that easy tonight. If you aren't coming through the main gate you either have to approach on foot, horseback or ATV, and out here you have to know the lay of the land or there's no telling where you'll end up. I sent a text to the owner of this property that I live on about the make, model and driver of the truck and started my background check. She'll be pissed when she realizes I went through her purse to get her identification, but I don't care. I needed answers and I couldn't wait for her to come out of her drunken stupor.

The information was easy to locate and her behavior tonight made a lot more sense once I got all the information. Reya Spencer is an RN from Texas who was severely injured in a motorcycle accident that claimed the life of her husband a year ago yesterday. According to her social media sites, she just got back from a European vacation her parents encouraged her to take after getting out of the physical therapy rehab facility a couple of months ago.

I glance over at the dark-haired beauty passed out on my bed and wonder what she's been through. I've experienced my own set of troubles over the last year and can't help but feel protective of her. It's stupid, considering I don't know anything about her that I haven't read online. She could be a raging bitch or a spoiled, uppity, money-grubber. There may not be an ounce of good in her and I might change my mind and want to turn her out to face that guy alone in a few hours when she wakes. For now, though, her history is enough to fire up all of my protective instincts.

For a few minutes, I study her. The clothing she's wearing isn't expensive. It's not cheap either, but it doesn't look as if she has a shopping problem. Even her suitcase had a minimal amount of clothing, all of it from middle-class retailers. Her limbs are long and a little too lean, not enough to make you turn away, but enough to make you realize she's had a rough year. There's a dark pink raised scar running from her collarbone up into her hairline. A couple of lighter scars under her chin are visible and one larger one on her cheek that I didn't notice last night. After reading the police report on the accident, I'm certain there are more to be found under her clothing.

Dark, thick eyelashes lie against her olive skin. One of her ears is exposed and has a slight point at the tip, almost like an elf. It's kind of cute. I know from last night that when those lashes lift they'll expose striking green eyes that have probably been making men stupid since she hit puberty. What could she have done in the little bit of time that she's been out of the hospital to have serious trouble following her from Texas to Florida?

An hour later Reya wakes, startled and a little freaked out. With no recollection of the events of last night, I wonder if she was drugged. It would explain why the guy was waiting outside. He thought she'd leave the bar ready to pass out and make his job a piece of cake.

"Easy, doll. I ain't gonna hurt you. I brought you here to protect you. Whatever trouble you're running from caught up to you last night and we had to get an escort out here to keep you safe. Tonight, I'll have to keep a closer watch on the property, but for now, you're okay. You wanna tell me what's going on in that pretty little head of yours?"

"It's not safe for you to have me here. I need you to take me back to my car. I'm on my own with this. Alex left me in a mess I can't seem to escape."

"Alex? Your husband?" Her eyes narrow on me and she takes a few cautious steps backward.

"Don't freak out. I pulled your driver's license from your purse and did a background check. I wasn't sure who I was protecting and thought it best to have a clue."

"You went through my stuff?"

"No, only your wallet so I could get your name for a background check. My buddy piled your stuff in your suitcase, but he didn't go through it, and we brought it with us. You need to call to check out of the motel and probably refold your clothes, judging by the way Hudson was shoving them in there."

"Hudson?" she asks, obviously confused.

"Hudson is my buddy. He's a member of Sunset Security—an elite protection agency—so I called him for help."

"Oh, that makes sense. Why are you helping me though? You don't know me. It seems a little weird."

"Where I come from, you always protect a lady. Doesn't matter if she's yours or not. Man's not a man if he walks away from a woman in need, and last night you were definitely classified as such."

"I remember doing a few shots, but I don't remember drinking enough to black out. I haven't done that since college."

"I think you had some help in that department. In fact, I'm sending one of the guys to the bar to talk to the bartender today to find out who else had access to your drinks. I bet if we ran a blood test we'd find out you had some sort of date-rape drug in your system."

Her eyes flash with a moment of fear.

"I didn't touch you except to carry you in, Scout's honor." I hold my hands up.

"I think I would be able to tell if I'd been violated. For some reason I trust you. It's what you said about the date-rape drug that has me freaked out." She plops down on the edge of the bed, resting her elbows on her knees and gripping her hair as it hangs down. "There's a long story here, one you don't want to be involved in. I can't go to my friends or family in Texas and put them in harm's way. This whole thing is a mess and I can't drag you into it."

I can hear the tears in her voice as she continues with her head down. "My house was ransacked while I was in rehab, so my family cleaned it up, thinking it was a random break-in. After I got out of rehab my family paid for me to take a trip across Europe, hoping to snap me out of my depression. While I was there my house was torn up again with the focus on the boxes from Alex's office. Nothing appeared to be missing, but everything was destroyed. This time they even tore up the canvas wedding picture that hung on the wall behind the couch. I'm lucky all my clothes weren't shredded, though his were.

"What they were looking for, though, I had with me on my vacation. It was amongst Alex's personal belongings from the accident. I requested they be released to Alex's father, who brought them to me at the rehab facility."

"How did the accident happen?" I don't tell her I've read the police report version.

"We were running from the guys who wanted what Alex had. Alex was driving like a crazy man, weaving in and out of traffic. He crossed a double yellow line while going around a curve and almost went head-on with a semi. Alex and the truck swerved, and we hit a tree. I don't remember any of that, it's like a big black hole in my memory. I only remember the conversation at the old gas station when he told me we were being followed. Someone we passed gave a report to the police about what they saw."

Dropping her hands, elbows still on her knees, she lifts her face and the tears are back. They're running so steadily down her face that they're dripping off her chin. I can't stand to see a woman cry so I cross the room and stand in front of her with my hand out. "Come on, doll," I urge.

She doesn't move, instead she studies me. I flick my fingers at her to come to me and she still doesn't move so I bend down and grip her wrist, pulling her as gently as I can to stand, allowing me to wrap my arms around her. She's stiff at first and I can't blame her; I *am* a complete stranger. I have some background information on her, but she doesn't even know my name yet. I smooth her hair down with my palm while she finally relaxes against me and cries harder. I'm certain there will be tears and snot all over my shirt, but I couldn't care less.

When she begins to quiet down, I say, "My name's Elias Covington. I'm from a little town in Alabama, but I live here now and work on this ranch with Bob Ives. If you want, I'll give you access to my computer and you can check me out. I was in the Army for ten years and when I got out I wasn't ready to go home."

"The guys that are after me are bad news. I'll only bring you trouble if I stay here. If you can take me to my car, I'll be on my way."

"You think you're safer out there on your own than you are here with me, behind the protection of the fences and my security system?"

"No, but if something happened to you because of me I'd never forgive myself."

I can't help the laughter that boils out of me. It's loud and long and I can't remember the last time I laughed like this. "Doll, look at me. I forgot to mention an obviously big piece of information. I was Special Ops in the Army. A Green Beret. I've survived shit a lot worse than this so don't worry about me. My friend Mike owns Sunset Security and he's agreed to help. It would be easier for us to do that, though, if we knew what you have that they want."

She cringes and lowers her eyes. "I still don't know how he got it, but I have a thumb drive that contains proof of these guys holding women captive and selling them off. When Alex died, we were on our way to meet with an FBI agent to turn it over."

"I'm guessing you never made it to meet the FBI agent?"

"No. After the accident, once I was lucid again, I wanted Alex's watch, so the Florida Highway Patrol released Alex's belongings to his father who brought the bag of stuff to me in the hospital. That thumb drive was in his pocket with thirty seven cents and a wrapped peppermint candy. No one else knew what it was for so they just passed it over to me in the bag that held his stuff.

"My house was torn apart twice because these guys wanted this thing. I took it with me to Europe, trying to decide what to do. I don't know what happened to the FBI agent. He didn't approach me while I was in the hospital so I don't know if he's involved, dead, or maybe never existed. I was scared to find out and unsure of whom I could contact with this information. I'm scared and I don't want anyone else to get hurt."

"Did Alex work with anyone?"

"Yes, his cousin and a secretary. They were tortured and killed while I was in Europe. My family didn't tell me because they thought it was a random case, and they knew I'd come home. They all wanted me to relax after what I'd been through. Those two moved to Dallas together right after Alex died, and parts of the city are rough so everyone chalked it up to city violence. As soon as they told me, I knew what happened and I freaked out. It's part of what sent me on the run."

"This is going to seem like an asshole question, but I have to ask. Is there any chance that Alex was involved in any of this?"

A single tear slips down Reya's face, but she wipes it away quickly. "No, Alex liked adventure and even had a small-time gambling business on the side, but he hated violence against women. I really think this is something he stumbled on and was just trying to do the right thing. I could be wrong, but I doubt it. I knew his shortcomings better than anyone, and he'd never take part in any kind of human trafficking."

For her sake, I hope she's right that her husband wasn't involved in something as sinister as this. Until I do some digging, I won't know.

## 4

---

## REYA

Normally I wouldn't trust a stranger to look after me. In fact, if it were a friend telling me this story, I'd tell her she was crazy if she didn't leave Elias and this town in the dust pronto. But there's something about him that makes me want to trust him. I don't know if it's his good-ole-boy southern charm or the fact that he probably saved my life last night. He could have done anything to me, as messed up as I was, but he didn't. Instead he chose the gentleman's route.

I sit on the love seat in his studio apartment and study him as he clicks away on his computer. Elias looks like he should be perched atop a horse on a cattle drive, with sweat on his brow and work gloves on his hands. The dirty white cowboy hat that hangs on the hook by the door matches the faded Wrangler jeans that hug his thighs and butt just right. I don't know the last time I noticed a man's butt that wasn't Alex's, but I can't help it, it's damn near perfect.

Worn brown cowboy boots sit over by the front door under his hat and I wonder if the leather is as soft as it looks. The navy blue plaid shirt he's wearing is ironed to perfection and tucked into his jeans. If I didn't know from our conversation that he was in the military, the ironing alone would probably have given him away, but the tucking in of his shirt screams military regimen. The blond day-old scruff growing on his face reminds me a little of Jax Teller from *Sons of Anarchy*, a favorite series of mine. I sigh and stand to stretch, ready to get more water. I can't get enough of it after my night of hard drinking. Elias seems to think I was drugged, but I'm not sure. It's possible I just drank way too much.

As I'm filling my cup I think about the fact that I haven't called my family in two weeks. I've texted them so they wouldn't call the cops and file a missing persons report but I'm sure they're still worried. Considering I haven't been the same since the accident, I think they're giving me more room to figure things out than they normally would, but it won't be long before they run out of patience. I guess I'd better call my mom at least. I move over to where my suitcase is sitting against the wall and unzip it. I dig the phone out of the compartment that I usually use for panties and socks, and power it on.

For the first time since I left Texas for Florida my phone lights up and immediately shows that I have over twenty unanswered text messages and an equal number of missed phone calls.

Finally, I dial my parents' number. My mom picks up and she sounds out of breath.

"Oh my God! Reya! I've been so worried. When your dad went by to check on your house there was a man inside going through your stuff. This is the third time since the accident. What's going on? It's obviously not a random break-in!" Her voice is near hysterical.

"Mama, calm down. I'm fine. I can't tell you anything about this because I don't want you and Daddy in danger. I'm getting help and hopefully this will be over soon."

"Reya, where are you? What the hell is going on? You can't

just tell me something like this and expect I'll say okay." She's crying now and it's getting louder. I can't deal with the emotional side of her. It's too much.

"Mama, if Daddy's home, please pass the phone to him. I love you, but I need to talk to him." There's a rustling on the other end of the line and my dad picks up.

"Sweet pea, where are you? What in Sam Hill is going on? We've been trying to get ahold of you for two days. We were ready to file a report with the police."

"All I can tell you is that I'm fine. I'm in a safe place with people who are going to help me. I can't tell you more or you'll be in more danger. Just trust me, Daddy."

"That's not a good enough answer for me. Your house has been broken into three times since Alex died and you took off out of here like a bat out of hell, with a shitty explanation. At first I chalked it up to you not coping well, but we're past that."

"Dad, I can't tell you any more than I have. This is bad, though. Bad enough that I know Derrick and Tory's murders weren't just city violence. All this ties into the same thing. I promise I'll explain, but not until I know this is done. I need to get off the phone. I love you and Mama and I'll call as soon as I can."

My father is not letting me out of this conversation that easy. "You don't have a choice but to tell me what's going on. Someone tried to break into our house yesterday and your mother was followed to the grocery store. We've already filed a police report about those two things, but I'm scared for you. And I'm scared to leave your Mama alone."

Oh God, I brought this to my parents' doorstep. Someone followed my Mama yesterday. The room feels like it's closing in on me as my dad continues. The roaring sound in my head is preventing me from hearing what he's saying. Within seconds the room is spinning and I can't seem to understand what's going on. The phone clatters to the floor as I fall down to join it. Elias must have seen it coming, because he was on his feet racing to me. He grabs me before I can hit the floor and lowers me down slowly. He shoves a pillow under my head while I lie there with the freight train in my ears and a fuzzy feeling all over. I hate these panic attacks. I've had several since the accident and they paralyze me.

"This is Elias. Who's this?" I can only hear his side of the conversation.

"I'm the guy who saved her ass last night."

"I'm trying to figure it out now."

"I didn't have to know her to know I wasn't leaving her in a dangerous situation when I have the means to protect her."

"My friends own Sunset Security, based out of Crystal River, Florida, and they're already onboard."

"Yes, sir, I said Florida. One of us will be in touch in the next couple of days. Make sure you're armed and don't leave your wife alone."

"Yes, sir. Army. Green Beret."

"Yes, sir. Elias Covington. I'll call when I have something. I'll do everything in my power to protect her, sir."

"You're welcome."

My vision is no longer hazy, but my heart rate hasn't slowed and my hands won't stop shaking. Elias comes into view and reaches out a hand to help me off the floor and onto the couch.

"Your dad's real nervous. He's scared for you and for your mom. I think we need to get this figured out so everyone will be safe."

I nod, unable to find my voice.

Elias returns to the couch and sits next to me with a glass of cold water. When my hand shakes so bad that water sloshes over the side, he takes it back and holds it to my lips to drink from.

"If I don't hold it, you'll be taking a bath in it rather than drinkin' it."

A small smile tugs at my lips. I shouldn't be smiling—even a small one—with everything going on, but I can't help it. I'm grateful for the slight humor and the fact that he's not irritated with me. Yesterday he was a normal guy, a ranch hand, going about his business. Probably no cares in the world. Today he's in the middle of protecting a crazy woman who can't even hold a glass steady. It's pathetic.

The smile fades from my lips and the tears pool in my eyes. These people killed Alex, almost killed me, tortured and killed Derrick and Tory, and are now stalking my parents. I'm holed up here with a man I don't know in a place I've never been. I want to scream at the top of my lungs until I have no breath left. My shoulders shake with the emotion that's taking over me and it's only a second before Elias wraps me in his arms and holds me tight while I cry. He strokes my hair like a child and whispers, "Shhh," over and over again. My tears flow for what feels like forever and when they're finally all gone and I'm sure there isn't an ounce of fluid left in me, I lift my head to find his intense sapphire eyes studying me.

"I'm so sorry. For all of this," I tell him as I sniffle. "You could die getting mixed up in this. I think I need to go home to my parents and work this out there. I don't want anyone else to get hurt."

"Doll, there's no way you're leaving my sight. Now that I know what these guys are capable of, I can't let you walk out that door until I know you're safe."

"But why? You don't even know me."

His brows pull together and he swallows hard. There is a long pause before he answers. "My little sister was raped and murdered in an alley outside a nightclub in Birmingham when I was in Afghanistan. I've always wished that someone would've helped her."

"Oh, Elias," I say, my heart aching for him. He swallows hard again and clears his throat.

"It's not something I can talk about." It's quiet between us for a moment until he continues. "I'm going to put my training to good use and call in a few favors. I'll do what I can to help you end this. How about you go get cleaned up and then we can tackle this problem head-on. I need to make a couple of calls. Do you remember what the FBI agent's name was?"

"The only name Alex used was Donovan. I don't know if that was his first or last or even his real name."

"Okay, towels are under the sink. Help yourself."

## 5

### ELIAS

Twenty minutes later, Reya comes out of the bathroom, her hair wet but combed, her face makeup-free, wearing a pair of sexy-as-hell yoga pants and a form-fitting workout shirt. Holy shit. For most women this is not the most attractive look, but on her... I'm almost speechless. I thought she had a nice ass, at least her jeans hinted at it last night, but those pants leave nothing to the imagination. It's perfectly round and firm and thoughts of bending her over the couch and smacking that thing before I... ugh, I need to stop this train of thought. Damn! I've got to get my head out of the gutter. This woman is in grave danger and obviously still stuck on her dead husband. It's too soon for her to even consider the kinky shit that passed through my mind just now.

Reaching down as discreetly as possible, I adjust myself and do my best to focus on the task at hand. I called my high school buddy who's now at the FBI and asked him to see if he can find Donovan. I'm sure it's like searching for a needle in a haystack, but it's worth a try. Until then I have to keep Reya safe and out of my twisted sexual fantasies. It's not like I'm hard up, it's only been a couple of weeks since I went home with a woman from the next town over. I've gone longer than that without sex before so this shouldn't be an issue. However, with her being as sweet and as beautiful as she is...it's a serious problem.

The waiting for information is killing me. As the day wears on I'm unable to concentrate on anything other than Reya. Every slide of her leg, flex of her arm, flip of her hair and sigh from her lips has my cock twitching. If I stay in this one-room apartment with her for one more hour, I'm likely to make a move on her she won't like.

"Reya, do you have sneakers or boots you can put on?"

Her eyebrows draw together. "Yes, why?" Even her voice is sweet, almost lyrical.

"I'm getting a little stir-crazy and thought we could walk down to the barn or tour the property maybe. I won't leave you here alone just in case, but I've gotta get outta here. Do ya like animals?"

For the first time since I saw her at Bud's Bar, her face lights up with an enormous smile. "I love animals. Especially horses. Do y'all have horses?"

"Yeah, this is a cattle ranch so we've got working horses. Do you ride?"

I stand and pull on my boots. Even though I try not to be obvious, I can't help but watch as she bends over her suitcase to grab socks and sneakers. God, that's the perfect ass. I probably should've made her change into jeans but I couldn't make myself ask.

"Only been on a horse once. It was part of an excursion on a Jamaican vacation, but I loved it."

"Well, come on, let's go see them. You can meet Walt—the ranch owner—while you're at it. I was stationed with his son in Afghanistan."

"Does his son work the ranch too?"

I pause, taking a deep breath. I've gotten better about talking about Lyle, but having to answer this question makes me pause every single time.

"No, he was killed during my second deployment."

Her hand covers her mouth and her eyes widen. "I'm so sorry. I shouldn't have asked." She lowers her head and walks to the door like she's embarrassed.

"Don't be sorry. Nothing we can do about it. He was a good guy and I hate to say it, but life goes on."

I grab my hat from the hook and place my hand on the knob to open the door when I feel her hand on my shoulder. A sizzling sensation spreads along my skin from the contact. When I turn to look at her she leans in and wraps her arms around my middle. I don't know if the hug is meant to comfort me or her, so I pivot, moving her to my front, and hold her close. How in the hell did I end up trying to comfort some woman I barely know? I'm generally not a cuddly type of guy, but I'm finding that I don't seem to mind it with her. It's possible...I even like it a little.

"I'm sorry," she says. "I'm so emotional with everything going on and I think it's beautiful that you're here with Walt."

I swallow hard and nod, ready to be done with this conversation. I might be comfortable holding this gorgeous woman in my arms, but I'm not about to cry all over her.

"You ready to see some livestock?" I ask as I finally open the door.

She releases her hold on my middle and gifts me with a small grin. "Yeah, it sounds nice. By the way, why do cowboys wear hats? I never have understood that."

"Keeps the top of your head cool and the sun off your face and neck."

"Why not wear a baseball cap or fishing hat?"

"I don't know about anyone else, but this was my granddaddy's. It's the only thing I own that matters. Just part of my history, I guess."

She doesn't ask any more questions after that.

This is a relatively large ranch, built by Walt's father over sixty years ago. My apartment sits on top of a storage area and both face the main barn, which houses twelve horses, about one hundred fifty yards away, across an open dirt area. Walt's main house sits off to the right and the driveway leading in and out of the property runs up the left side of my apartment. The smaller barn, or shed, where he keeps a lot of the equipment and the ATVs is behind the main barn. The rest of the property is surrounded by pastures of varied terrain.

We approach the main barn and Walt saunters out and takes a second to assess Reya, his face blank. When I called him this morning to explain the situation, he didn't give me a hard time. He just said to let him know if he could do anything. I wonder what he's thinking.

"Hey, Walt. This is Reya." He pulls off one of his work gloves and reaches out a hand to shake with her. She clasps it and says, "I'm sorry I brought all this drama to your home. I hope to be out of your hair soon. Can I do anything to help you in the meantime?"

I'm unable to hide my surprise as I turn toward her. She wants to help with something? I can't picture a beautiful woman like her working anywhere on a ranch. Her offer cracks the hard exterior of the old cowboy. "No ma'am. And don't apologize. Sometimes we can't help the things that happen to us. I think it's a real good thing that it was Covington who was there to help. If anyone is equipped to deal with something like this, it's him." He nods in my direction.

"I can't thank him enough for stepping in. I'd probably be dead if he didn't help me."

Uncomfortable with the fuss they're making over me, I reach for her hand and say, "I'd like to take one of the ATVs out and show her the property if you're okay with that."

"Sure, son, whatever you want to do."

"First, she wants to meet the horses."

Pushing his glove back on, he nods in the direction of the barn. "I'll leave you to it then," he says.

"It was nice meeting you, Walt."

"Likewise, young lady."

After we enter the barn I lead her down the long row of stalls, half of which are empty because the other ranch hands already have the horses out on the property somewhere. My favorite horse, the one I always ride is Sampson and he's watching us over the top of the door. We step inside and I reach up to stroke the side of his neck. "Hey, Sam. You miss me today?"

Almost as if the horse understands what I asked, he swings his big brown head in my direction and chuffs in my face, causing Reya to jump back a little.

"Relax, he likes to give me lip from time to time. He's harmless as long as you stay away from his back legs." She scoots in closer to me and gently strokes the beautiful animal in front of us. I glance at her and for the first time since we met, Reya is calm, peaceful even. We stay with Sam a few more minutes before I lead her to the small barn where we keep the ATVs. I snag a key from the shelf where we keep them and sit astride the nearest ATV. When I look over to help her on I find her frozen in place, staring at the four-wheeler like it'll bite her. Her olive skin is ghost-white and I realize quickly that she may not be able to do this. Fuck! I can't believe I didn't think of it. I'm so insensitive. Sitting on the back of this thing is similar to being on a motorcycle, and judging by her response she hasn't been on one since the accident.

I remove the key and swing my leg back over, ready to ditch this horrible idea and borrow Walt's old 1940's army jeep. Reya continues to stare at it, or right through it. Afraid she's lost in a memory and not wanting to hurt her further, I say quietly, "Come on, doll. I wasn't thinking. We'll go get Walt's jeep."

Her wide eyes swing to mine, like my voice snapped her out of her thoughts. "I can do it," she croaks. "I know I can, it just might take me a minute."

"You don't have to, though. I don't mind. I wasn't thinking of anything but fresh air when I decided this. The jeep is fine." Why doesn't she understand that I don't want to hurt her and this is clearly hurting her?

"No. I want to do this. I *need* to do this. It's not even the same thing so I don't understand why my stomach hurts."

"Are you sure?" I ask, still thinking this is a bad idea.

She nods and glances back toward the machine.

"Okay, I'll get on and wait. You join me when you're ready. If you change your mind, it's okay."

Her eyes close and she swallows hard. I straddle the ATV again and wait. She doesn't make me wait long. There's an audible intake of breath before her warm body slides in behind mine. She wraps her arms around my middle and rests her cheek on my back. Why does that have to feel so damn good? I reach down and cover her clasped hands at my middle and squeeze. I know it was hard and I'm proud of her for trying even though it's probably the last thing she wants to do.

"Ready?" I ask.

I feel her nod but she stays quiet.

"Hold tight."

She squeezes almost too tight, but I take it slow at first, circling both the big and small barns twice. By the time I head for the south fence she loosens up a little and after about ten minutes her hands relax enough to rest right along my hips, not even joined together anymore.

"You alright back there?" I yell.

"Yeah, I'm good."

I smile and hit the throttle a little more. The first time we encounter a series of bumps and bounce around a little, she clutches tight around me again, but the next time she actually giggles. Knowing she's no longer holding on for dear life or gasping in fear, but laughing and finding enjoyment with this gives me a sense of pleasure I'm not familiar with.

We take a turn to the east side of the property and I pull up to the highest hill, where a spacious field of wildflowers looms in the background of a good stretch of Walt's land. It's the most beautiful place on this property. When I park and kill the motor, I tell her, "Let's stretch for a few minutes." She climbs off and I follow, but stop dead in my tracks when I realize her ass, in those amazing yoga pants, is right in front of me. Grabbing distance. Smacking distance. Caressing distance. My blood moves south to a region of my body I don't want it in and I groan. I'm not a teenage boy. Why does just the sight of Reya's ass have me sportin' wood in the middle of the afternoon?

She glances back at me and I move up by her, but angle away a little so I'm standing next to her, eliminating any chance she can see the bulge in my jeans.

"It's beautiful here," she whispers.

I turn to look at her and realize she's right, but I'm not thinking about the landscape. It's her. Her long dark hair is pulled over one shoulder and her eyes sparkle a little in contentment. The smooth skin of her face and neck, despite the long scar on one side, has me dying to see what's underneath her clothes. She licks her bottom lip, which I now notice is slightly smaller than her top and I find that I can't tear my eyes away from it. What the hell is wrong with me? This woman lost her husband in the most horrific way and is running for her own life. She's not thinking of all the things I could do to her out here in the middle of nowhere or back at my place in the dark of night, so why am I?

I'm a twisted fuck. That's why.

## 6

## REYA

Elias might be the sweetest, most genuine guy I've ever met. Not to mention attractive. His personality, though, is what's making it hard to separate things in my head. The southern gentleman thing has me melting like chocolate in the sun. Add to that the blue eyes, blond hair and muscles, and it's almost too much. I must be nuts. I'm in the middle of fighting for my life, but the only thing I can think of is what he tastes like. His mouth, his skin, his—

"Come on, climb up here," he says, snapping me out of my wicked fantasy as he climbs up on top of a huge boulder. My face heats up, embarrassed like maybe he can read my thoughts when I know that's not possible, thank goodness. It's been so long since I've been held, even longer since I've been kissed and much longer since someone has taken me to bed.

When I look back on things, I realize Alex was distant for several months leading up to the accident. I blamed myself for working too much, but when I sift through the memories now, knowing what he was dealing with, I understand it wasn't all me.

After the accident, when I was recovered enough to actually mourn him, I got angry he didn't tell me something was going on sooner. I was furious he put us in danger and allowed all our future dreams to be torched. I'm still not certain I'll ever forgive him.

"You okay?" Elias asks, the deep timbre of his voice bringing me back to the here and now.

"Yeah, just thinking." I turn around in place, absorbing the breathtaking scenery.

I can tell he's looking at me when he asks, "What are you thinking about?"

*Be bold, be brave*, I tell myself. *Live a little. This may be your last chance.* Sucking in a deep breath, I turn toward him, allowing my gaze to travel up his body before I meet his eyes. "Things I've got no business thinking about." How I said that without blinking or looking away I don't know. Tiny butterflies take flight in my chest as his eyes darken, their focus shifting to my lips. I lick the lower one nervously and hold my breath.

Taking one step closer to me, he asks, "What kind of things?"

It's been awhile since anyone has flirted with me. My scars and sad face scare men away and before that Alex did so I'm not 100 percent sure he's flirting but I'd like to think that's what's going on.

I close my eyes for a second before finally releasing the breath I'm holding, opening them again as I exhale. "You."

His eyes widen just enough for me to give away his surprise by my confession. "Me? Why?"

"Because I really want to do this." I rise on my tiptoes and press my lips to his. Damn, his lips are incredibly soft and full. I didn't expect them to feel so good. When he doesn't react, embarrassment floods my system and I pull away quickly, taking a step back and slapping my hand over my mouth. "I'm sorry," I mumble, realizing that I misread the situation. The lack of reciprocation indicates that he's not interested. He didn't want that at all and now my flight instinct takes hold. I need to get out of here. I turn and spot the ATV, remembering that I have to ride all the way back with my body pressed to his. I'd rather crawl in a hole out here and die from a bear attack. Clearly, I didn't think this through.

"Hey! Wait." He grabs me abruptly and turns me to face him. He searches my face and his brows pull low over his spectacular eyes. "Why did you do that?" he asks.

God, this couldn't get more mortifying if we added an audience. I shrug a little and try to yank myself free of his grip.

He holds a little tighter, not painfully so, but tight enough that I'm not going anywhere without serious effort. "Seriously, why did you kiss me? I need a reason, Reya."

His insistence in discussing this, is embarrassing me further and making me angry. I didn't peg him as the cruel type.

"Why does it matter? I said I was sorry," I snap at him.

"Because it does. I don't want you thinking you owe me anything, because you don't. I'm not that kind of man."

*What?* "You think I kissed you because I thought I owed you something?"

He nods. "I know you're still not over your husband. You've been through a lot and it's been intense…"

Is he crazy? I'd never use my physical affection to pay someone back. I can't decide if I should be mad or offended. "I kissed you because I wanted to. Even with all the shit I have going on, all I could think about was what you'd taste like. Okay? Does that make you happy? Are you pleased you made me look like an idiot?" I yell.

Before I have a chance to move further away from him, he yanks me forward as his mouth crashes to mine, and I melt as soon as his tongue slips between my parted lips. He pulls back just a little and whispers, "Been thinking about more than just what you taste like. Kiss me back, doll." That little bit of knowledge sends my brain spiraling to the land of lust and sweaty, wild, mind-blowing sex. When his lips meet mine this time, I open and devour him, making sure to memorize every stroke of his tongue, every change of direction, every nip of my lips with his teeth. It's by far the hottest kiss I've ever had and I've had some hot ones.

Within a few seconds, his hand slides down over my ass and squeezes, and I don't expect the groan that comes from him. He breaks the kiss as he squeezes again. "Best fucking ass I've ever seen," he mumbles before he resumes kissing me, this time with one hand on my ass, the other shoved up under the hair of my nape. Parts of me that have long since been dormant light up like the Fourth of July.

My hands grip the hem of his shirt, ready to remove it when a shot rings out, hitting a spot probably only two feet from us. He breaks the kiss and pushes me down to the hard surface, covering my body with his. Another shot rings out to the other side of us and he angles off of me a little. Then he starts shouting, "Go, go, go!" and pushes me toward the ATV. I scramble down the boulder toward the waiting four-wheeler. Two more shots zip by. I see him stumble and clutch at his thigh, and I scream. He manages to get on the ATV and as soon as I wrap my arms around his middle he hits the throttle causing me to grip tight so I don't get thrown off.

We're zipping through Walt's property as fast as this thing will carry us. The roar of the motor isn't enough to drown out the sound of shots hitting trees and rocks all around us. Elias weaves us through a narrow passage of trees that climbs higher and suddenly drops about four feet. I scream and squeeze him tighter. Somehow we land on all four tires and take off again. We're not returning the way we came, we're going through a huge thicket of trees and I'm terrified we'll smash into one, so I close my eyes and drop my head. We hit a bump, jolt sideways and my eyes fly open. It's at that point I notice the huge blood stain on his pants from his lower thigh downward that seems to be building by the second. We've got to get somewhere so I can stop the bleeding.

As we clear the tree line, the back side of the barn comes into view and I realize we lost them, but Elias doesn't let off the throttle. When we barrel around the corner he finally slows and enters the barn. Bill comes in right behind us on foot.

"What the hell happened? I got a radio call from Johnson that he heard shots fired on the east side of the property."

Elias taps my thigh and I dismount to stand unsteadily on shaking legs, but he doesn't move. The only words I can seem to utter are, "He's been shot."

Walt's eyes grow round and he does a quick scan from head to toe, pausing on Elias's leg.

"Damn. Let me help you off that thing and I'll see if I can get Doc out here. Until then, I'm calling the boys in to stand guard. You need to call Mike and his guys and tell them what's going on."

"We're going to need more help than I previously thought," Elias confesses.

Walt turns and jogs out of the barn as I help Elias to a bench against the barn wall. There's an awful lot of blood, but being a nurse, that part doesn't bother me. I hate that it's his blood, so much of it, but thank goodness it doesn't make me squeamish.

"Got a pocket knife?" I ask him. His eyebrow rises, he's unsure of me wielding a knife. If the situation wasn't so scary I'd probably laugh at him.

"For your jeans," I answer his unasked question as I get on my knees in front of him. I shake my hands out, willing them to stop trembling.

"I'm not sure I want you near my leg with a knife and shaky hands. Besides, I think it's just a graze. It burns a little, but that's it. If it was worse, I'd know."

"Not necessarily. Adrenaline has a way of masking the worst pain."

He sighs and grumbles, "Fine, just don't cut my leg off." He pulls the well used pocket knife out and places it in my palm.

As carefully as I can, I slit up the outside of the jeans and peel the blood-soaked material back. Thank goodness he's right. It's just a graze on the lower part of his thigh. He may need a couple stiches or butterfly bandages, but it didn't bury itself in the muscle like I was afraid of.

I look around the room until I finally spot what I'm looking for: a first aid kit. I jump up and hurry over to the dusty old box. It must be fifty years old. I open it as I return to where he's sitting, pulling out the sterile wipes. Thank goodness they're still damp and I'm able to spend a few minutes cleaning the area around the wound.

While I'm working on his leg he calls his friend Mike to explain what's happening. I gather from Elias's side of the conversation that Mike's rounding up some men to stand as our security guards. I can't believe the lengths these people are going to, to help me when they don't even know me.

By the time Mike arrives, my shaking has subsided and I'm calm again. When did I become a woman with the strength to get up and keep going in the midst of danger? Hell, when did I become the woman in danger? I've always been a good girl, so to speak. Never finding trouble and steering clear of those who did. It's clear I can't claim that anymore.

Elias stands to walk out of the barn and cringes. When I slide up under his arm to help brace him while he walks, he practically growls at me and shifts away. My feelings would likely be hurt if it weren't for the fact that Elias is obviously a man's man and wouldn't in a million years let anyone see a weakness.

Two armed men, one with a pistol and one with a shotgun,

escort us to and up the stairs to his apartment. Once we're inside, one of the men stays outside and the other joins us inside, standing by the door. Mike's seated at Elias's table, typing on a laptop, and looks up at us.

"Hey, man. You okay?"

"Just a graze. Looks worse than it is."

Mike glances at me.

"I'm a nurse. I looked at it and he's right. Probably needs a couple of stitches, but otherwise it should be okay."

Mike looks thoughtful as he nods.

"I'm going to the restroom," I tell the men, getting the feeling they'd like to talk without me in the room.

"Okay," they respond in unison as I exit.

I brace my hands on the sink, stare into the mirror and review the last hour. Between the kiss, the extreme sexual tension and someone trying to kill me, I'm overwhelmed. Emotionally wiped out. I must finally be out of tears though because I don't cry; I just allow the heavy weight of all these things to settle on my shoulders as I wash my hands.

When I come out of the bathroom Mike is gone and an older gentleman with a white handlebar mustache and white hair cropped short against his head, who I'm assuming is Doc since he's looking at Elias's leg, glances up at me.

"You clean this up and put the butterfly bandages on him, young lady?"

I move closer and look at the leg. "Yes, sir. When I'm not running from men with guns, I'm an RN."

"Hm. Well, you did such a good job there's nothing left for me to do," he grumbles.

Is he angry I did his job? I was just trying to get Elias through until the doctor could get here.

"Wipe that look off your face, I'm not mad 'bout it. Just surprised. Not many nurses running around these parts. I'm leaving you some fresh bandages and some ointment, you obviously know what to do. Call me if you think I need to take another look," he tells me as he stands and gathers his stuff. He grabs his hat off the hook next to Elias's hat, gives us both a chin lift and walks out the door.

I pick up the supplies and move them to the bathroom, and when I return Elias is stretched out on his bed, with his eyes glued to the television angled in his direction. While I was in the bathroom before Doc arrived, he must have changed out of the nasty jeans. Now he's lying in a pair of shorts and a clean T-shirt. One hand is tucked behind his head while the other rests on his stomach. It looks like it's a lazy football Sunday afternoon for him. Not like we just survived being shot at and chased across the property. Unsure of what I should do, I walk over and sit on the love seat and fiddle with the hem of my shirt. This is kind of awkward.

"Come here," he commands.

I lift my head, surprised by his words and look around like maybe someone else is in here.

"Yes, you. Ain't no one else in here, doll."

I walk over and sit on the bed, angled to face him, next to his hip. "How do you feel?" I ask.

"I'm okay. The question is, how do *you* feel?"

"I'm fine. Thank you for saving me." One side of his mouths tips up. He doesn't respond to my comment. Instead he taps the bed beside him, on the side opposite his wounded leg. "Want to lie with me for a bit? We've got guards outside the door."

Warmth rushes through me at the thought of lying in bed with him, possibly snuggled up. There's no way I'm passing up this opportunity. "Yes, okay." I walk to the other side of the bed and crawl up next to him. His arm is stretched out, indicating he wants me to lie against him. As soon as I settle and his arm wraps around me, I breathe a sigh of relief. That small thing of being wrapped up in a man's arms, especially one who's as strong as and looks like Elia is amazing. Comforting, tender, and safe. Perfect following the events of the afternoon. It doesn't take long for me to doze off.

It's dark out when I awaken to the thrashing body below me. "Elias?" I ask hesitantly, unsure of what's going on. He doesn't respond, but continues to flail and twist like he's trying to get away from something. A pained sound escapes him, the kind I've only heard an injured animal make. I panic, hating to see him struggle. "Elias!" I say, just short of a yell, while I shake his shoulder. His body settles a little so I try it again.

He shoots up into a sitting position as his eyes fly open, wild, afraid, and shocked. His head swivels as he takes in the setting. I know that fear and the complete disorientation that comes from waking from a night terror to find everything around you normal and quiet. I've done this very thing hundreds of times over the last year. It's a horrible feeling trying to separate a dream from reality, especially if the dream is part memory.

When his eyes lock on mine and he registers me, he moves fast and the next thing I know, I'm on my back. Before I can say a word, his hips are between my legs and his mouth is on mine. At first I'm too surprised to react, but as soon as his tongue breaches my lips, I open for him. He flexes his hips into me and I can feel his erection grow between us in the few seconds it takes me to engage. I bend my knees, press them against the outside of his rib cage and shove my hands up under his shirt. While my fingers explore his bare skin, I become impatient and tug his shirt off. His hips continue to grind into me while his mouth consumes me. My pulse kicks up higher. I'm panting as he breaks the kiss and drifts down my neck, planting kisses every inch of the way, and I almost melt when he takes special care along my neck scar. The heat of his breath along my skin singes in the sexiest way. I want him. No, I need him and if he comes to his senses and stops this, I'm probably going to have a serious breakdown. He shifts down my body, stopping to suck on my nipples through my T-shirt and bra. "Eliassss," I hiss.

The further down he goes, the more I squirm. The more eager I become. He jerks my shirt up roughly and I wiggle and maneuver until I get it all the way off. I can see his hungry expression in the dim light of the television still flickering in the background, and I've never felt sexier or more wanted. With a swipe of his fingers he frees my breasts from the cups of the bra and spends a few minutes teasing me with his teeth and tongue on each one.

"More," I groan as I grip his hair with my fingers and hold him to me. The pulsing between my legs has hit epic proportions just from his work at my chest. Even the slightest touch to my clit is likely to send me off like a rocket.

His lips trace a trail to my breastbone and slowly down my belly. I squirm and beg for more as he tugs my panties off. With his face so close to my sex, impatience takes over and I lift my hips, offering myself to him readily. "Please put your mouth on me," I beg as I stare down my body at the sexy cowboy between my legs. There is a wicked grin plastered on his face as he dips a little closer. The warmth of his breath against my most tender area, before he's even touched me, is more than I can take and I buck slightly. God, I need it now! He clamps down on my thighs with his rough, strong hands, keeping them open, to hover above my pussy, teasing and taunting me. How can I be this close to orgasm and he hasn't even actually touched me between my legs? I'm going to explode.

"Tell me you want this, that you want me, doll."

"Yes, yes, yes, I want you," I pant.

"Say my name. I need to know it's me you want."

Is he kidding? Who else would I want? The man working me into a frenzy, teasing me, is the only man in the world I want. I lift up on my elbows, making sure he can see my face clearly. The sight of him between my thighs is wildly erotic. I lose focus for a second until he kisses the lips of my sex like he would my mouth as he returns my stare.

"Elias. You're the one I want. The only one I can think of. Please, this is torture." The whiny quality to my voice is embarrassing, but damn, I'm so ready to go I'll get on my knees and beg if he wants me to.

His grin has me sucking in a breath. "You're beautiful," he tells me, before he buries his face in my pussy and laps at my damp center. One swipe of his tongue across the tight bundle of nerves has me crying out. This is vicious torture and beautiful bliss all at once. With special concentration on my clit, he flicks his tongue rapidly. I'm pinned to the mattress, squirming and screaming his name. The guys we have posted outside will probably be breaking the door down any minute to save me.

"More," I holler, and he gives it to me with that wicked quick tongue. When I don't think I can take another second, he sucks my clit into his mouth and I come, screaming his name while thrashing wildly against him. I'm probably bruising his mouth.

Instead of sliding up between my legs and having sex with me, he rolls to his back and flops with his hands above his head. That's not what I expected and I'm a little concerned that I hurt him or did something wrong. Oh, my gosh. What if he's sorry he did this with me? What if he hated my reaction? Maybe it was too much. How embarrassing. What if that was a pity thing or he was half asleep and... I can't even finish the thought. The humiliation will likely kill me in the daylight.

His breathing is heavy and I chance a glance down his body. His cock is hard, pushing against his shorts. If he's still hard why wouldn't he continue? I can't take the wondering so I ask, "Are you sorry you did that?" My voice is soft, but it seems loud in the quiet room. I'm glad he can't see my face clearly when he shifts to his side to look at me.

"No, never. I'm sorry I practically attacked you."

"You wanted it?" I ask to confirm trying to understand.

"Since the moment I saw you at the bar."

Relief floods my system and I sit all the way up and attempt to tuck myself back into my bra.

"Take off the bra, Reya," he tells me, his voice hoarse. Since it's the last piece of clothing I'm wearing, I take it off and toss it to the floor. Then I crawl over to him, my hair hanging forward, almost in my way. I sit back on my heels, pull my hair to one side of my neck and allow my eyes to roam from his sexy disheveled hair to his bare feet. "Take off your shorts, Elias."

"You don't hav—"

"Take them off," I'm stern as I cut him off.

For a few seconds he studies me and must be okay with what he sees because he lifts his hips and shuffles them down his legs avoiding his injury. I scoot in close and run my fingertips along his hardened shaft. He's probably average length, but his girth is off the charts. I've never been with a man that thick. It's quite simply... breathtaking. He shudders at my touch. I wrap my palm around his heat, not coming anywhere close to having my fingers touch. I'm suddenly a little nervous I won't be able to get it in my mouth. "Jeez," I breathe.

His stomach muscles jump a little as he chuckles. Pre-cum leaks from the tip and I swirl my tongue over it to taste him before I take the head into my mouth. His skin is hot and smooth, soft velvet over steel. My lips stretch as I work my way down, bobbing, taking a little more each time. My jaw aches with every inch I take, but I won't stop. I want to give him the beauty he gave me. I keep a firm grasp on him, stroking slowly, and dip my face further between his legs to take his sac into my mouth and suck gently. He opens his legs a little more to give me room and I hum appreciatively. He squirms and I can feel his thighs tense up. That's something he really likes so I repeat it. He reaches down and knocks my hand out of the way to stroke himself, like he can't delay any longer. I want to be the one to give this to him so I take back over with my mouth, moving his hand away. Hollowing out my cheeks, I increase the suction until my jaw aches. He's so wide it's hard to keep my teeth covered but I do my best. The vein on the underside of his cock begins to pulse under my tongue and I know he's close. Gently, I palm his balls and find them pulled tight so I work him fast and hard, allowing his hips to thrust, fucking my mouth steadily. The more he gets lost in it the more it hurts because he's so damn thick, but I'm determined. He grips a chunk of my hair and tugs to remove me but I keep going.

"I'm gonna—" He doesn't finish because I press on the area right below his balls and he goes off like a fountain, coating the back of my throat. He doesn't groan through this or call my name or grunt. No, he roars. It's the most manly, animalistic sound I've ever heard and it has me working harder to drain him fully. When it's finally done, I release him, sit back and lick my lips.

In one quick, surprising move, he sits up, wraps one arm across my chest and pulls me down to the bed, landing half on me. There's a soft touch of his lips to my shoulder, another on my collarbone, one more on my neck and then his mouth is on mine. This kiss is gentle and sweet. It almost feels like it's a thankful kiss.

"You might want to let the guys guarding the door know I'm not dying. At least not in the murder sense of the word, more in the orgasmic kind of way." He laughs and drops to his back, maneuvering us both to the way we started the night.

"We need to check your wound. Make sure it didn't tear

open. You were thrashing around when I woke you up. Are you okay?" He runs his free hand through his hair and holds it there.

"I'm fine. I get the dreams from time to time. If I had you to wake up to every time though, I'd be much better." After a few quiet minutes, he asks, "Are you sure you're okay with this?"

I love that he's being such a gentleman about it. "More than okay. I needed that. More would've been good, but nothing could make me regret what we did."

"I don't want to take advantage of you," he whispers, running his fingers through my hair.

"I haven't felt this wanted or safe in a long time. I don't feel taken advantage of."

He doesn't say anything, but he holds me a little tighter until we both drift back off to sleep.

## 7

## ELIAS

I wake up before Reya, with the taste of her on my tongue and the scent of her sweet pussy lingering under my nose. I don't think a woman has ever come that hard for me. I thought she was beautiful before, but now I know she's downright scorching without clothes on. I can't imagine how much better it would be with her taking my cock. I can't wait to see her expression when I stretch and fill her. Morning wood is the worst. Not only is it uncomfortable, but it prohibits me from thinking of anything other than how to remedy it. I shift, ready to slide out from under her and jerk off in the shower when her arm that's across my middle clamps down to keep me from moving and her hand drifts lower to squeeze my rock-hard cock.

I was so lost in the fantasy of sex with her I didn't realize her breathing had changed and she'd woken up. I don't even think her eyes are open yet. Her hand slips down further and palms my balls, and I groan. Some guys don't like their balls touched. I'm the guy who likes them tickled, fondled, licked and sucked. Her thumb strokes across the soft skin and I fight to stay quiet. That feels fucking fantastic.

Reya's hair falls forward and brushes my chest as she rises

up a little to place a kiss on my nipple. I do my best to hold still and enjoy whatever she has in store for me but when she takes my nipple between her teeth and tugs a little, I grip her hair and pull. I've always enjoyed some pain with my pleasure and she's hitting all the right spots. I don't think she's ready for more than oral with me and I don't want to lose control and spook her.

"Slow down there, tiger. You're about to get more than you bargained for if you keep doing that sexy shit with your mouth."

Her right eyebrow rises like she's indicating a challenge accepted. She pushes her hair over her shoulder and straddles me, never taking her gaze from mine. Her pussy hovers close enough that I can feel her heat, but not close enough to feel her wetness. It's psychological torture knowing that heaven is so damn close, but not quite there.

She holds her left hand out to me, "Condom."

When I don't answer right away, her right hand slips down between her legs and her knuckles graze my dick as she slips one finger inside herself. I don't take my eyes off of what she's doing. It's hot as hell. I don't want to look away so my hand smacks at the night table, feeling around for my wallet. When I finally grasp it, I fumble until it's open and pull out the condom, placing it in her still outstretched hand. She closes her fingers around it and lowers that hand to her thigh while she continues to finger herself. Meanwhile, my cock is still nestled between her thighs with zero penetration for me and I'm ready to explode.

"Reya," I grit out between clenched teeth.

"You like this?" she asks as she removes her fingers and slides them higher to circle her clit. I can't even answer I'm coiled so tight with need, ready to beg her to stop teasing me. As she continues to touch herself, I grip her hand and peel the condom away. "Do you want it or not? I can't hold out anymore."

"What if I say no?" she asks, her tone teasing.

"Then I guess you'll be watching me jerk off because I can't wait another second."

Her eyelids lower halfway and her eyes roll back a little. "I'm so close, give me one second," she confesses, her voice breathy.

Fuck, she's killing me. I rip the foil open and roll the condom on. When I'm removing my hand, her thighs grip me tight and her body shudders, making her glorious breasts shake. Gorgeous. I flip her to her back as fast as I can and rest my cock at her entrance. "You want me or not, doll?"

An aftershock rolls through her and she shivers. "Yeah. I want you, but I think I need a minute." Her lips are tipped with a slight grin and I know she realizes I'm on the edge.

Wrong answer. I flex my thighs and push inside her perfect, tight heat and groan. Holy shit she's tight and still rippling from her orgasm. Pulling out slightly, I rock in again and although she's wetter, the fit is still tight. I won't last long with all the teasing before and the tightness she's giving me now. I pull out and dip my head to pull one of her beaded nipples into my mouth, teasing it with my tongue. Then I switch to the other. When I'm done, I kiss my way across her chest and suck on the soft, creamy skin near her nipple, leaving a hickey behind. I smile at my mark and thrust back inside of her. She glances down and sees the beginning of the red mark. "Elias, you can't leav—"

I thrust harder and pick up my pace, effectively stopping her rant. Her back arches off the bed as her pussy clenches even tighter. I can feel it flutter right before she screams my name again. The guys on the overnight shift are probably hating me. Listening to another dude have sex isn't high on any man's priority list when you can't have any yourself.

When her legs relax and slide down a little, I hook them with my arms and practically fold her in half to finish. I thrust harder and harder until I finally come, growling her name.

Damn, she feels good. I stroke in and out of her until I'm finished and then I leave the bed to dump the condom. When I return she's on her side, curled up tight. I pull the hair away from her neck and kiss it softly. That's when I hear her sniffle. She's crying? Fuck! This is what I was afraid of. I've either hurt her physically or this was too soon for her.

"What's wrong? Did I hurt you?"

She shakes her head but doesn't speak.

"Are you sorry we did that?"

"No, it's just..." she pauses and sniffles again. "That was the first time since Alex, and I didn't think I'd ever have that again. And it was so good and I don't know how to act now." Her crying grows louder so I fit myself to her backside, curling in tight and wrapping an arm around her.

"You're not sorry?"

"No," she whispers, "are you?"

"Hell no, I'm not sorry," I reassure her. "You should act however you need to act. I'm not going anywhere." I lay a series of soft kisses along the scar at her neck before I nestle into her and wait for her to settle down.

How in the hell am I going to let this woman go back to Texas once we get her shit sorted? The way I feel right now I'll probably jump in my truck, drive straight through, kidnap her ass and drag her back here.

After a few minutes, she settles and I ask, "Why did you come to Florida?"

"I've always wanted to come to Florida and this rural part of the state seemed like a good place to hide. I have no family or friends anywhere near here so no one else could get hurt if those guys found me. It wasn't the best idea. It was the plan of a panicked crazy person."

"So you got in your car and drove until you hit this town?"

"Sort of. I took every back road between home and here,

stayed in my car at a couple of rest stops, and drove until I found Martha Ann's Motel across the street from the bar. It was the anniversary of Alex's death and I wanted a few drinks and an actual bed. That seemed like a good spot. I can't believe they found me."

"Were you using a credit card?"

"Of course, I didn't pull out cash until I was at the bar when I realized they didn't take credit cards. A single woman on the road with a wallet full of cash? That's asking to be robbed."

"But a credit card makes you traceable. Even a low-level hacker can track your movements by where you use your credit card. Don't you watch TV?"

"Shit. That explains an awful lot. Rarely do I watch television. Netflix mostly. Alex only watched sports and I wasn't home enough. Well, sometimes if he was in the shower I'd turn on a show about women looking for crazy expensive wedding dresses just to bring a dose of estrogen to the house, but Alex would always change it back."

I'm not sure how to respond to that so I don't.

She must need to talk because she continues, "I found out when I was recovering that he was betting on the side. Actually, he was a small-time bookie. I had to have Derrick, his cousin and assistant, clean that mess up for me. I didn't understand it and had no idea who he took money from, who he owed, or anything. Apparently, there was a lot I didn't know about my husband."

"Do you think that has anything to do with the guys after you?"

"No, that all got cleaned up. It took my entire savings to do it, but that's all square. Thank God for the insurance settlement or I wouldn't have a dime to my name."

"When we get this settled, are you going back to Texas and back to your job?" I hold my breath, waiting for her answer. I shouldn't care. I don't know her, beyond what I found on the internet, the sunshine in her smile, what her pussy feels like wrapped around me, and the fact that a whole shit ton of trouble has accompanied her to Montana. But if I could decide for her, I'd ask her to stay for a little while just to see...if maybe there is something there for us.

"I don't know. There are certain aspects of my job I can't do anymore. I have a lot of back pain if I stand for long periods of time and I don't have the strength I once had to physically handle patients in a hospital setting. I love nursing, but I need to find a new way to do it, I guess."

A knock at the door forces me out of bed. I shuffle on a pair of jeans and open the door. Out of the corner of my eye I see Reya pull the covers to her neck and I smile a little to myself.

"Hey, man. Sorry to bug you, but Hudson called me when he couldn't reach you to let you know they have information for you. They're on their way here now."

"Thanks. We'll get dressed. Let me know when they arrive."

"No problem," he says with a smirk as he glances over my shoulder. He no doubt heard what we were up to a little while ago. I close the door.

"You might want to get a quick shower. My friends will be here in about fifteen minutes to talk to us about what they found."

She nods and scoots off the bed, dragging the sheet with her to keep covered. I'd love to tell her not to bother with that, but I know we need to get dressed and back to reality.

THIS TIME I HEAR THE TRUCK APPROACH AND STEP OUTSIDE TO greet Hudson and Mike with a cup of coffee in my hand. "Ya'll want a cup?" I ask the two men who had the night shift.

"Nah, I'm meeting my wife for breakfast and will get one

there." The other guy shakes his head but doesn't say anything more. I'm used to guys like him. I served with a lot of them who'd rather grunt than talk most of the time and that's fine with me.

"Morning," Mike says while Hudson talks to the guys who stood watch all night. They wave and hurry to their trucks without another word.

"Come on in. Reya should be out of the shower in a minute and you can tell us what you found."

As Reya's coming out of the bathroom there's another knock at the door and I open it to find two more of the Sunset guys. I let them in and the one closest to me nudges me with his elbow. I scowl at him because he's smiling at Reya like she's this morning's breakfast. *I don't think so.* I glance over at Hudson to find him grinning like an idiot. Not because he's also undressing her with his eyes, no, he's committed to his wife, Stacey, but because he must have heard from his men about my morning activities.

"Hey, guys," Reya greets everyone. She gives them a shy wiggle of her fingers and turns to me with a little blush to her cheeks as both men grin at her.

Mike clears his throat to end the uncomfortable silence, and says, "Why don't we sit down to talk. Guys," he points to the newest Sunset men and continues, "I need you to secure the perimeter. Keep your eyes peeled. No one except Walt Ivy or our guys gets up here."

They nod, flash one more smile at Reya and leave the room.

Those of us who remain pull up chairs around my little table and Mike begins. "I called an old friend at the Bureau and had him do some digging. At first, Donovan didn't mean anything to him. Which didn't surprise me since we didn't have anything more than the name Donovan and because there are over 35,000 people working for the FBI. Luckily, with the human trafficking subject matter, we were able to narrow it down to thirteen possibilities. Only one of those was working in Texas and under investigation for bribery. His name was Matthew Donovan. A thirty-five-year-old white male from Tulsa, Oklahoma."

"You said *was*," I note.

"Yes, he was found murdered on the side of the road in Gainesville, Florida, on May 10, 2016."

Reya gasps and we turn to look at her. All the color has drained from her face. She moves the hand now covering her mouth and says, "That was the day of our accident. The day Alex died."

"From information gathered by the investigators, two guys were suspected, but nothing could ever be pinned on them. They're brothers—John and Chris Backowski—from a bad part of Detroit, who were involved in a gang that specialized in selling flesh. The notes on the case say the brothers bailed in the middle of the night two years ago and tried to start their own operation in El Paso. When my buddy dug into the case Donovan opened on them, he found notes about evidence that Alex Spencer somehow acquired. Supposedly the proof in his possession was enough to send these two to prison for the rest of their lives."

I cock my head to the side, trying to understand this. "You're telling me that two street thugs are behind all of this? Not a whole organization? Not the mob or a gang? Just two guys?"

"Yes, that's exactly what I'm saying."

"So why hasn't anyone done anything about them? It's been a year since Donovan was killed. This is crazy."

"Other cases had higher priority."

"I think I need to see what's on this thumb drive. I can't believe I haven't asked to see it before now."

I pull my laptop out of the case and open it in front of me, powering the machine on while Reya grabs the thumb drive. She's quiet as she passes it to me. There are a series of video files with time and date stamps on them. The quality isn't great, which means this was filmed using shitty equipment, by someone who didn't know what they were doing. My guess is it was Alex or his cousin Derrick.

When I click on the first file there's no sound, but it tells me everything I need to know. The bile rises in my throat because I saw something similar in the middle of a raid in Afghanistan. In this video, there are a group of five men. Three of them are in expensive suits, walking around a warehouse containing several large cages. The two other men, in baggy jeans, flat-billed hats and baggy T-shirts, stand off to the side like they're waiting. When the suited men approach the men in baggy jeans there's lengthy conversation and it's then that you see movement in the cages. You can't make out faces but they're the size and general shape of women.

The recording cuts out shortly after that so I open the next one. It's a similar situation, but different men in suits. I go through each video file on that drive and each one shows the same thing. Sometimes it's different men in suits, sometimes it's the same.

The last file shows when the cages are opened and twelve women in handcuffs are led out. They file out of the room under heavy guard. It's definitely human trafficking.

How in the hell did Alex get these? Was he part of this? It's a big leap from a bookie who sells real estate to selling people. The dates on the files are three months before Alex's death.

I run my hands through my hair and grip the back of my neck, trying to decide how to proceed from here. We all sat and watched this. We all know what this is. It's obvious why these guys want this thumb drive. If it got into the right hands, these guys would never see the light of day outside of prison, and since they aren't part of a bigger organization they have no one on the inside to make it go away.

"Alex did this?" she asks, her breathing rapid like she's going to hyperventilate.

"I don't know if he was involved, but he has proof of others who are. This is bad and it explains a lot. Now I know why they didn't just pick you off in the parking lot outside the bar. That guy needed to get to you to find out where this file was. If you die they have to start the search over. I'm pretty sure that's why they tortured Alex's staff before they were killed."

"What if he was part of this? Everything I knew about my husband was a lie. I'm not sure how I mesh this new information with the man I thought I knew. The Alex I loved would never allow this to happen to innocent people, especially women. I want to puke." Her hands cover her stomach and her focus moves to the floor.

"Don't read into any of this until we can figure out what side of this he was on."

"Does it matter? The whole thing is horrible. Even if he was on the right side he didn't do anything to save the women in the videos."

"Hey, look at me." I squat down in front of her determined to calm her down. Her eyes meet mine. "Don't let this tarnish his memory until you're certain it should. We don't know how he collected this or what he planned to do with it."

A single tear falls, rolling down her cheek and dripping off her chin. She swipes at it and sniffles. "What do I do now? It's only two guys. How do we get them? I don't want to run anymore, but more than anything I want the truth."

8

—————

## REYA

While the men decide what to do, I sit on the couch with my legs folded under me, reviewing my life with Alex in my memory. He changed some those last few months, but I can't wrap my head around the idea that he may have changed enough to allow this to happen. There has to be a good explanation and I need to know what it is. I don't know how long I sit there, but I feel the couch dip next to me and turn to find Elias sitting there. The frown lines on his forehead and around his mouth are prominent as he studies me.

"Are you okay?"

"Not really. I knew this was ugly, but I'm afraid of what I'll find when the truth is revealed."

"I'm sorry. I know this is hard."

"That's an understatement. Did you guys figure out what we're going to do?"

"We're going with simple. We're going to sit and wait. They're desperate enough to come to you. All you need to know is that I'm going to stay with you until this is over. I won't leave you alone, but they're going to come for you. So we're going to be prepared."

"Is this going to work?"

"They need what you have. There are only two of them and there are at least ten of us. Can you shoot a gun?"

"My dad's been taking me to the gun range since I was eight or nine years old. So, yeah. I'm best with a 9mm or a .38 special, but I can shoot just about anything."

"Mike's going to go back to his place and pick one up for you. We all have our own. Once he's back and you're armed, the Sunset guys are leaving."

"They're leaving?" I can't hide the fear in my voice.

"Yes, but they aren't going far. They're going to circle back and approach from different points on the property. The Backowski brothers will think it's just us and make their move. They've proven they aren't afraid to do that when it's just you and me. Walt found where they came in last time so we left it open and plan to allow them to come back through that way."

"We're sitting ducks?" My insides twist and churn.

"Yes, and no. We'll have backup. They just won't be sitting outside the door to protect us. It's going to be okay. I trust the Sunset guys with my life."

I nod because I don't have anything else to say.

"These guys are the experts and if this is what they think is best, I'll go along with it. We're also giving Mike the thumb drive. His friend at the FBI is going to take it into evidence. If they have it they can get arrest and search warrants on all their properties. There is no reason for you to have it anymore. Are you okay with that?"

I nod. He's right. I don't need it. I have help and they're going to put an end to this one way or the other.

———

WITHIN A COUPLE OF HOURS MIKE AND THE BOYS HAVE COME AND gone. I've got a loaded 9mm on the table next to me and Elias is armed too. I've never been patient or one to sit and wait for something to come to me. I'd prefer a "let's go get them" attitude, but the guys are right. The Backowski brothers are desperate enough to come for me and they're obviously tired of waiting.

For the next several hours we watch television, play cards and finally stretch out on the bed. Neither of us could sleep if we wanted to, but we're trying to follow normal patterns so if they're watching and waiting they won't realize anything is going on.

When we lie down on the bed, he pulls me in close so I can rest my head on his chest. He kisses my hair before he asks, "How are you holding up?"

"The best I can." I can't think of a better answer. The truth is, if someone dropped a safety pin on the floor I'd jump a mile in the air, but there's no point in telling him that. He can't fix it.

"You're so strong, Reya. I don't think I've met a woman stronger than you are."

What do you say to that kind of compliment? Nothing seems appropriate so I stay quiet. He positions his fingers under my chin and lifts it so I'm looking at him. Of all the things that have been so horrible about this experience, I do have my time with Elias to be thankful for. He's reminded me of what it's like to be alive, both physically and emotionally. Why can't a man like this live in Texas? Maybe there is one, but it's not him, and after this it's going to take me a long time to get over Elias Covington, my cowboy hero. His quiet, gentle but strong manner is the polar opposite of Alex and exactly what I've needed. There could never be another Alex for me, but there could be someone else. I just don't think I'll want anyone else when this is said and done. I'm already half in love with Elias as it is. Maybe it's because he rode in on a white horse to save me and has risked his life to protect mine ever since. Maybe it's because the sex is hotter than sin and the tenderness in between is so fulfilling. Or it could be because he doesn't need to fill the quiet moments with endless chatter or television. He's content to relax and enjoy the peace. Maybe it's just everything that is Elias Covington.

I lean in and place a soft, tentative kiss on his lips and pull away to look into his eyes. They're amazing, twin cerulean pools of perfection. I could stare into them for hours if it didn't seem creepy. He slides his fingers into the hair at my temple and pulls me to him. This time he kisses me. It's equally as soft as mine was, but he slips his tongue between my lips and coaxes mine to join his. As the kiss grows deeper, I swear I fall further in love with him.

How do you fall for someone you just met a few days ago? I never believed it to be possible. It took me months and months of dating Alex before I felt a fraction of what I feel now. Could it be because I'm so vulnerable? Or because this whole scenario is supercharged with emotion? Instead of analyzing it, I think I'll enjoy it before I have to give it up.

Keeping hold of me, he rolls us so I'm on my back, but never breaks the kiss. We make out like teenagers, kissing and groping with hungry abandon for a long time, until he pulls away.

"God, I want to make love to you so bad." He punctuates the statement with a kiss to my lips, my nose and finally my forehead. "But I won't be caught with my pants down when these two bozos show up at the door." I grin at him. The mental picture is a funny one.

"You can still kiss me though, right?" I ask, not wanting it to end.

"If that's what you want, doll."

This time I thread my fingers into his soft hair and bring his mouth to mine to resume the hot and heavy. I make sure to absorb everything about this moment so I can bring it out when I'm back in my bed alone in Texas.

A little while later we've worked ourselves up into a nice frenzy. It's so bad for me that I'm grinding on his thigh looking for relief. I should be embarrassed, but I'm not. I'm too turned on to be. It's in the middle of this when he pulls away. "Shhh," he whispers.

I lie still and try to hear anything over the pounding of my heart. Elias jumps off the bed and tugs on his boots. "Get your shoes on and get your gun. There's a rope ladder under the bed. Grab it and wait." He shoves his gun in the back waistband of his jeans and I do the same. Quickly, I tug on my socks and shoes while he runs around looking out each window. I pull the heavy rope ladder out from under the bed and when I stand up I understand why he wants it. Fire. I can see it out all the windows except the kitchen one and the heat level in here is rising.

"Come on, these assholes are burning us out. Promise me you'll shoot to kill if they get to us and I can't do it. It's us or them and I want us to walk away."

I've never killed anything in my life except the occasional squirrel that ends up under my tires, but I won't have a problem aiming at these two jerks. "I promise."

We open the kitchen window, hook the ladder on the edge and drop it down. This is not going to be easy, but we need to move fast or this place will collapse. "You're going down first, be ready to jump and run toward the barn if they aren't there."

I nod, scared to death, and begin my descent. As soon as I hit the ground, Elias starts climbing down and I turn to run, only to be hit around the middle with something hard. It knocks the breath out of me and takes me down. I didn't see the guy waiting in the shadows for me. I must have caught the guy in the guts or the nuts when I went down because he's rolling around next to me. I scramble to my feet fighting to catch my breath, ready to run, when he grabs the hem of my jeans and pulls me to my knees. A shot rings out and I turn to see the guy holding me go limp. I don't wait to see where he was hit, I run as hard as I can for the stables. Another shot is fired but I don't turn around to see who it is. Footsteps come up hard and heavy behind me and I glance back to find Elias on my heels.

We are halfway to the barn when all the horses gallop past at full speed, obviously spooked. Elias and I dive out of the way to avoid being trampled by a couple. Another shot spooks the horses and Sunset guys come out of the woodwork to help lead the horses to safety. Elias tugs me to a standing position and pulls me toward the back side of the barn when more chaos unravels. The gate to the cow pen opens and cattle rush out, filling this part of the property. Havoc reigns and with all the enormous, terrified animals running around, it's obviously not safe.

Walt yells over the noise behind us, "I can't find Sampson!"

Sampson is Elias's horse. We have to go in after him. I don't ask, I just turn and run inside.

"Reya! Wait!" Elias and Walt are both yelling at me, but I don't stop. I don't want anything to happen to the horse because of me. "Reya!" It's total mayhem everywhere. Horses, cows and men all running amuck. There's fire engulfing the storage area underneath Elias's house and now the actual house too. This is out of control. I can't focus on any one thing or even seem to think straight.

When we get through the barn doors he takes the lead and we're almost to Sampson's stall when the gate is flung open and a gunshot spooks him out of there. Elias throws me to the ground, out of the path, and falls on top of me with a heavy thump to protect me. Once the horse has passed he leaps to his feet, and as he's helping me up a man appears behind him and swings a crowbar hard at his back. Elias stumbles and growls in pain but turns and charges the man. The guy swings again, catching Elias in the shoulder hard and I'm shocked Elias doesn't fall to the ground. Elias hits him in the waist with his uninjured shoulder, like a football player, taking them both down.

The crowbar drops next to them. Because the two men are wrestling, kicking and throwing wild punches, I can't get in there to grab the crowbar. It's the most vicious fight I've ever seen. I'm so stunned by the encounter I can't decide if I should stay and help Elias or run. Where would I run to at this point? I could get trampled outside the barn and I don't know where the other brother is. The man, now on his back, is taking a serious beating. Somehow though, he manages to grab hold of the crowbar and swings it down hard on Elias's head before I can warn him. Elias goes limp immediately and I stand stunned, terrified that the asshole killed Elias. How could he live through a head injury like that?

I don't come to my senses quick enough and the guy grabs me hard by the arm and tugs me toward the door, cussing the whole way. When we make it out the door he stops and shouts, "Johnny!" toward the lifeless man on the ground about a hundred yards away. The brother on the ground doesn't move. "Johnny!" he tries again. I do my best to wiggle out of his grip while he's slightly preoccupied. This only pisses him off because he squeezes my arm harder and yanks my hair with the other hand.

The one who I now know to be Chris Backowski—since his brother Johnny is lying on the ground in the middle of the mess they made—spins me around, releases me, and backhands me all at once with what feels like the force of five fists.

I drop to my knees and he screams, "You killed my brother, you crazy bitch!" and hits me with a closed fist this time. I fall to my back, stunned by the pain radiating through my cheek, and watch as Chris straddles me, wrapping his hand around my throat.

"Where the fuck are those files! I need the fucking files! All you had to do was give them to me. Instead you got your new boyfriend killed and made me drive down here to the middle of fucking nowhere. Alex was a dumb motherfucker so I'm assuming you're just as stupid."

He's squeezing my throat harder and I instinctively reach up and grab hold of his wrists as I try to free myself, but he's too strong. It feels like my eyes will pop out of my head and my throat is burning.

"That fucker thought he'd be smart and video our operation and then blackmail us. He was making a ton of money off of us and probably would still be alive, but he grew a conscience and went to the Feds. That was an easy fix but we never could find those damn files. Where the fuck are they?!" he leans in and screams, spitting all over my face. The more he loses his mind the tighter his grip gets, while my vision grows hazy with each passing second. Pretty soon I'll either be unconscious or dead.

In a last-ditch effort, which he's too busy choking me to notice, I let go with one hand and clumsily yank the gun out of my waistband, sliding off the safety as I bring it around. I can't breathe. I'm never going to be able to do this. I kick with my legs, trying to dislodge him and he lets up just enough for me to get a breath before he's squeezing again. This time I let go with my other hand, moving the gun between us. I pull the slide back to chamber the round and turn it into his gut. I don't think about anything but breathing again as I fire bullet after bullet into him. His eyes widen in shock, his grip loosens from my throat and then to my horror, he collapses on me. I can feel his warm sticky blood coating my shirt and I freak out, bucking and squirming. There's a dead guy on me! He's so damn heavy and I can't get him off me. "Help!" I scream, completely undone. "Help! Help! Help!"

Within seconds he's yanked off me and tossed to the side.

Hudson stands above me, out of breath, dirt streaked face lined with concern. He helps me up and I take off in a sprint to where we left Elias on the barn floor. Behind me I can hear the apartment collapse in a cacophony of crackles, crashes and pops.

The sound freaks me out but I don't have time to look back. I need to know if Elias is dead. His body is so still and there is blood pooling on the ground. Putting my fingers to his throat I search for a pulse and thankfully it doesn't take long to find it. It's still strong and steady. He's just knocked out. I run my fingers over his face and head gently and find the knot where he was hit when he went down.

"Is he okay?" Hudson asks from behind me.

"He's breathing and has a pulse. It's likely he has a concussion, but he's at least alive."

"Are you okay?"

"I'm fine."

I can hear his footsteps retreat as he initiates a phone conversation.

The adrenaline slows and my body becomes weak so I rest my head on his chest and listen, gratefully, to the beat of his heart. It doesn't matter that I'm soaked in someone else's blood or that my body hurts all over or that all my clothes just burned in a fire. The only thing I care about is that this man is alive and breathing.

9
——————

## ELIAS

When I came to, I was on the barn floor with Reya curled up to me. Being a little disoriented, I freaked, thinking she was dead because she was so still. But as soon as she lifted her head I calmed down.

The next several hours consisted of firefighters, policemen, the coroner and emergency personnel coming and going while asking a ton of questions. It was exhausting and I could tell Reya was ready for it to be over. A year-long nightmare for her can finally come to a close and she can get on with her life. I should be happy I helped and that she's okay, but instead I feel hollow. I remember this feeling well. It took over my life after I got out of the military.

My home and all my belongings are gone, not that it was much, but it was still mine. The peace I'd worked so hard to gain since I came here went up in that same puff of smoke. Reya stumbled drunkenly into my life a few days ago and twisted it inside out. I never thought about loving someone again. Never thought about making a commitment again until those last moments before all hell broke loose last night. She was already getting under my skin before that. She's beautiful, strong, resilient, loyal, and intelligent. Who wouldn't want a woman like that at their side? Maybe if there was no chemistry I'd feel differently. But we have that in spades.

Something passed between us on that bed last night, something I didn't even know existed. Now, I have to let her go. It's time for her to move on with her life, and with all of this tied up and her questions answered, she can.

Earlier today her father flew in to the airport in Tampa and Mike picked him up. I didn't want her driving home alone, especially after everything that's happened and she refused to let me help. I can't lie and say that didn't hurt, but I wasn't going to admit it out loud.

Her father, Jeb Saunders, is a large, robust man with a kind smile and firm handshake. In fact, when I met him upon his arrival, he almost shook my hand right off as he thanked me for everything. Walt put us in his guest rooms in the main house an hour ago and I've been lying here trying to figure out how to say goodbye and let Reya go. I've also tossed around the idea of asking her to stay and finding us somewhere to live nearby, but I quickly realized how selfish that would be and let the thought die.

The creak of the door snaps me out of my thoughts and I glance over to see Reya tiptoeing in and closing it behind her. Without a word, she slips into bed and straddles me. My hands slide up and clasp her hips automatically. *What's she doing? Why is she here?* She hasn't said much to me since her dad arrived so I thought maybe she was ready to be done.

Reya dips her head in close and brushes her lips with mine. When she sits up she whips her shirt over her head and rocks a little against me. I stifle a groan as I grow with the friction. She leans down again and slips her tongue between my lips. Her mouth is minty and warm and I get lost in the sensation of her. When I can't get any harder, she raises up and strips off her panties and tugs my boxers down and off. Then she sits up, opens a condom packet and rolls it on me. Considering my apartment burned to the ground, I have no idea where she got it, but now isn't the time to ask. Now is the time to enjoy the feel of her sweet pussy wrapped around me and her nails buried in my chest as she rides me. Her hips rock slowly at first, steadily increasing the pace until I'm forced to hold the headboard so you can't hear it squeaking or banging against the wall.

Her beautiful breasts bounce and sway in time to her movements. I wrap my free hand around one and roll the berry tip between my fingers, causing her pussy to clench and her head to roll back. Strands of her long hair brush my thighs behind her. I want to shout her name, but instead I grip her hips and hold tight as I climax so hard it feels like I've emptied myself completely. Her body shudders and she whimpers as her orgasm hits her seconds later. Finally, she collapses on my chest and rests there. She doesn't say a word and neither do I. How do I make this last longer, like all night?

Reya draws designs on the skin of my shoulder with her fingernail as I rub her back softly.

"I'm going to miss you," she whispers. "Tomorrow I go back to my life, but I'm not ready to leave you."

There are two things I want to say to her. One of them being that I want her to stay. The other that I'm in love with her. But knowing those aren't the right things to say to her I remain quiet. After ten minutes, she kisses me one last time and climbs out of bed, looking for her clothes.

As she's shrugging her shirt back on I finally say her name.

She kneels on the bed and kisses my lips. "Shhh. You don't need to say a thing. I get it. You don't owe me anything," she whispers, then leaves the way she came. And I'm right back to the empty feeling I had before she came in here. What the hell is wrong with me? Why didn't I say what I'm feeling? Probably because it's wrong to try and keep her here. This is not her home.

THE NEXT MORNING, I FOLLOW THEM OUT TO THEIR CAR AND shake hands with her dad before he goes to the driver's seat and leaves me with her.

"Thank you for everything. I'm so sorry about your house and your stuff. I wish you'd let me repay you."

Reaching out, I push the stray strands of hair over her shoulder and out of the way. I could say they were in her face, but that would be a lie. The truth is that I wanted to touch her at least one last time.

"It's all stuff. None of it mattered. You're safe; that's what counts. You don't owe me anything. Walt will get the insurance check and rebuild. I'll find myself a place in town. Everything's okay. Just go home and be happy. That's all I want, is for you to be happy. You deserve it."

We stare at each other for a long time and I can feel all the things I pushed down last night creeping to the surface. Almost as if she's saving me from myself, she breaks the stare-down and hugs me. I hold her tight and kiss the top of her hair. Finally, she pulls back, turns and strides to the car. "Reya!" I call to her like I'm going to say more. But of course I don't—I can't—so she climbs into the car without another look back. I wave as she disappears from the property, taking the last little bit of my heart with her.

## 10

### REYA

I've been back for three weeks and haven't slept for shit. I accepted a job right after I got home at the same hospice house I worked at before the accident, and I started a few days ago. Sadly, I'm not the least bit excited about it. In fact, I'm not excited about much of anything these days. I've been staying with my parents until I can sort out where I want to live, and although that's fine, I can't seem to make myself even look. It's pathetic.

Most days my mind lingers on memories of my time in Florida. About the way the field of wild flowers stretches along Walt's property or the sound of the cattle as they graze nearby. I swear I can still smell the mix of hay and fresh, humid air, and I miss it. It only took a few days for me to fall in love with rural Florida and Elias Covington. I miss him more than any of the things that I miss about Florida, though. I miss the look of him in his Wrangler jeans and that dirty cowboy hat that he loved. I really miss the quiet, deep timbre of his voice and the warmth of his arms. I won't mention what I miss when the lights go out.

I wanted him to ask me to stay, but he didn't. For a few seconds I thought he might, but I was wrong. I almost wondered when I left if what I was feeling was an illusion. It's easy to get wrapped up in emotion when life is in turmoil like it was. Add life or death situations and a sexy hard-bodied man and I think it's impossible not to get carried away. I thought once I was home I could forget him. The problem is...I haven't. In fact, it's worse now.

Men don't fall in love after a few days, especially with women in situations as crazy as mine was, so I'm sure he was happy as hell to see me go. Sure, there was sex involved and men love that, but I think he's the kind of guy who is happier alone, and I was stomping all over that.

Last week I bought him a brand-new, sexy white Stetson hat and shipped it to him with a thank-you note. I can never replace his granddaddy's hat that he lost in the fire, but I could at least get him a nice replacement. I just hope he likes it.

It took me forever to write the note I put in the box, and I must have used a hundred sheets of paper trying to do it, but I finally settled on simple.

*Elias,*

*I can't thank you enough for rescuing me and ending my night-mare. I'm so sorry your granddaddy's hat is gone. I know this won't replace the sentiment of your old one, but I hope you'll be able to make use of this one.*

*Thank you doesn't seem like a sufficient term to say to someone who flipped your world upside down. But I'll say it anyway because I'll never be the same. Thank you.*

*With a grateful heart,*

*Reya*


It wasn't my best, but I didn't want to look at that hat for one more minute and think about the super soft hair it was going to cover, or what he'll look like wearing it, so I put it in the mail last week.

We were low on milk and eggs when I left for work today so I stopped to pick some up on my way home. Now I'm headed to my parents' house for another night in front of the television watching game shows and the Hallmark Channel. Ugh.

As I turn down their street I notice a big white truck in the driveway. My heart skips a beat when I realize the tailgate is down and a good-looking cowboy, wearing the sexiest Stetson hat I've ever seen, is sitting on it. *Oh my God! What is Elias doing here?*

I pull in behind my dad's car and throw it in park. My heart has picked up the pace and is hammering in my chest. I blink a few times and make sure I'm really seeing what I think I'm seeing. He's still there, studying me through my window. Looking more handsome than I remember. His light blond hair is curling along his collar and ears a little, but he's freshly shaven. His Wrangler jeans are obviously new but I bet they fit the same as the old ones.

When I climb out of the car, it's like I'm in slow motion. I'm afraid to hope that he might be here for me, but I'm also not going to ignore the possibility that he might be. Why else would he be here?

I stop about two feet in front of him, afraid that if I get any closer I'll leap right into his arms whether he wants me or not. "You're here," is all I can say.

"Yeah, thought you deserved a thank you for the hat and I suck at writing letters. It's easier for me to do it in person." The sound of his heavy southern accent melts my insides. His lips twitch and one side rises in a half smile.

"You drove all the way here to say thank you?"

He cocks his head to the side and pauses. "Yes, and to tell you I miss you."

My heart is now thundering in my chest loud enough that I bet he can hear it and I reach up to rest my palm on it like I can calm it down that way. I wish I could come up with something good to say, but I can't get a single word to form. Realizing I'm not going to be able to talk, I instead close the distance between us and throw my arms around his neck. He wraps his arms around me and lifts me up higher.

"You miss me too?" He pulls back to pin me with those gorgeous blue eyes.

When I nod a yes, happy tears spill over my lids.

"Let's not do that anymore then," he says, referring to my crying, as he wipes the tears away. He kisses me hard and long. This kiss is inappropriate for the front yard of my parents' house, but I don't give a damn. He breaks away and rests his forehead against mine.

"Your Mama said you got a job."

"Yeah," I answer as I glance down at my scrubs.

"If you can give me a few weeks, so I don't leave Walt without help, I'll move down here to be with you. That is, if you want me."

"You'll move your whole life for me?"

"This is probably the best time in my life to move, considering I only have about a week's worth of clothes and no furniture to my name." He grins like this is funny.

"Do you *want* to leave Florida?"

He tucks a stray lock of my hair behind my ear and smiles sweetly at me. "I want to be wherever you are."

"Are you sure?"

He gives me a look like that's a stupid question. "Reya, it took less than a week to fall in love with you. I can't imagine what a lifetime will do. I don't care where we are, as long as we're together."

"Then let's go back to Florida. There's nothing here for me

except my parents, and they can visit. I don't know what I'll do for work, but I can figure it out."

"Funny you should mention work. Doc called me last week asking if you'd want a job as his nurse. He said it would be in the office and out on house calls. I told him you went home and I think he got mad at me."

I laugh out loud for the first time since I was with him last and his eyes smile back at me.

"Florida it is." I pull him down for a kiss and when I break it I say, "And for the record, I'm pretty sure I fell in love with you when I got a view of you in those Wrangler jeans the first time." He laughs as I smack his ass and drag him toward the house.

# ACKNOWLEDGMENTS

Teddy, Mykenzie, Tristen and Cassidy your support means the world to me. Thank you to Judy Swinson and Kat Mizera for always encouraging me.

To my TLC Crew, as always, what you find is what you find. Love you guys!

Heather Finley and Katie MacGregor thank you for the polish and shine!

www.ingramcontent.com/pod-product-compliance
Lightning Source LLC
Chambersburg PA
CBHW072033150726
47999CB00002B/887